Boo and Baa
Have Company

Lena and Olof Landström

Boo and Baa
Have Company

Translated by Joan Sandin

R&S
BOOKS

Stockholm New York London Adelaide Toronto

It's autumn. The tree has dropped its leaves.

"Phew," says Boo, "what a lot of leaves!"
"And they all need to be put in the compost pile," says Baa.

Boo goes to get the wheelbarrow.

"It's squeaking," says Boo.
"We need to grease the wheel," says Baa.

Baa gets the oilcan.

She greases the axle.

"Now it meows when I push it," says Boo.

"It meows when you're standing still, too," says Baa.

Boo and Baa think this is weird.

"A cat!"

"It's afraid to climb down," says Baa. "We must help it."
"We can tempt it down with some fish," says Boo.

Boo opens a can of sardines.
"Let's hope it's hungry," says Baa.

"It's not hungry," says Baa.
"What do we do now?" Boo wonders.
"Let's try a plank," says Baa.

Boo and Baa get a plank from the basement.
They push it out through a window.

"It doesn't dare go onto the plank,"
says Baa.

Good thing there's a ladder handy.

"Now it dares go onto the plank!" shouts Baa.

"Lousy ladder," says Boo.

Boo can't get down. "I'm hungry," he says.

"I'll be right back," says Baa.

To be on the safe side, Baa makes lots of sandwiches:

a cucumber sandwich,

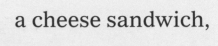
a cheese sandwich,

a tomato sandwich,

an egg sandwich,

and a sardine sandwich.

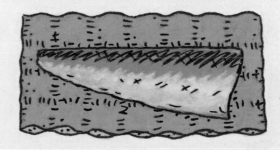

Baa ties a rope to the basket.

"Watch out!"

The basket is heavy.

"Yummy!" says Boo.

Now the sandwiches are all gone.

"Tie the rope under your arms and I'll
lower you down," says Baa.

"Now!" hollers Baa.

"Help!"
Baa is lighter than Boo.
She hasn't eaten any sandwiches.

It's lucky there is a pile of leaves.

"Now let's go inside and get the cat," says Boo.

But when Boo and Baa get inside, the cat is back
in the tree again.
"Maybe it *wants* to be up in the tree," says Baa.

"Let's leave the window open, just in case," says Boo.

It's nice with all the fresh air.
Boo and Baa are sleeping like logs.

Also by Olof and Lena Landström

Boo and Baa in the Woods
Boo and Baa Get Wet
Boo and Baa at Sea
Boo and Baa on a Cleaning Spree
Boo and Baa in a Party Mood
Boo and Baa in Windy Weather

Will Goes to the Beach
Will Goes to the Post Office
Will's New Cap
Will Gets a Haircut

Four Hens and a Rooster

Rabén & Sjögren Bokförlag, Stockholm
www.raben.se

Translation copyright © 2006 by Rabén & Sjögren Bokförlag
All rights reserved
Distributed in Canada by Douglas & McIntyre Ltd.
Originally published in Sweden by Rabén & Sjögren
under the title *Bu och Bä får besök*
Text copyright © 2006 by Lena Landström
Pictures copyright © 2006 by Olof Landström
Library of Congress Control Number: 2005936302
Printed in Denmark
First American edition, 2006
Second printing, 2007
ISBN-13: 978-91-29-66546-8
ISBN-10: 91-29-66546-9

*Rabén & Sjögren Bokförlag is part of
Norstedts Publishing Group, established in 1823*